To Janice

MORROW JUNIOR BOOKS / NEW YORK

MOLLY BANG

Delphine

It's from Gram!
She's sent me a present,
and it's waiting at the
Post Office.

I think I know what it is. I'm *sure* I know what it is. But I'm just a little bit worried.

I don't know if I'll
be able to steer it.

And I'm afraid
I might fall off it.

And I'm scared
it will go too fast
and I won't be
able to stop it.

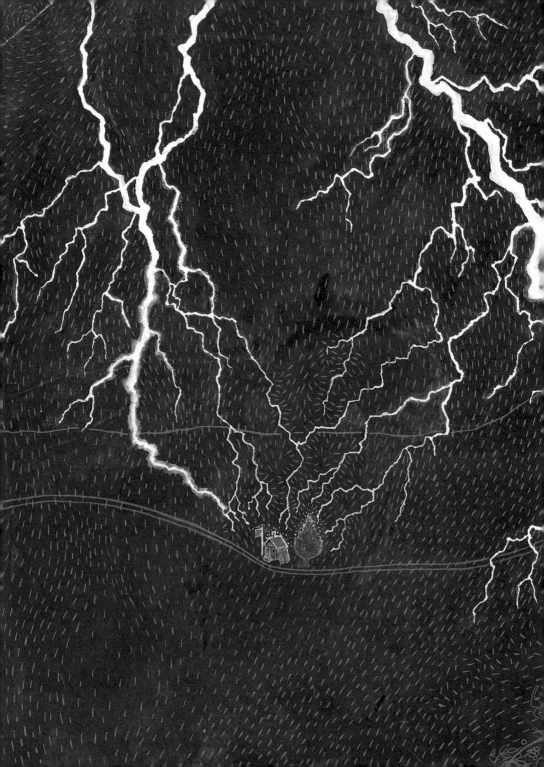

I'm *terrified* of it!

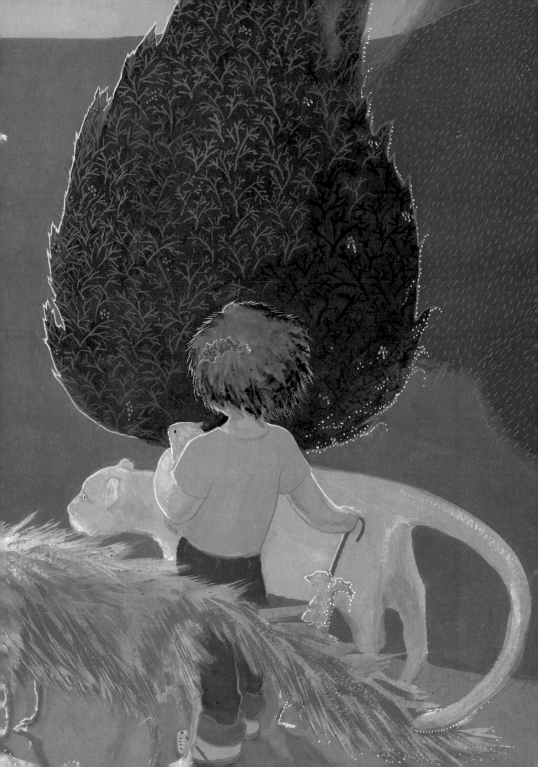

Printed in Hong Kong.
1 2 3 4 5 6 7 8 9 10
Library of Congress Cataloging-in-Publication Data
Bang, Molly. Delphine. [1. Gifts—Fiction] I.
Title. PZ7.B2217De 1988 [E] 87-34958
ISBN 0-688-05636-9
ISBN 0-688-05637-7 (lib. bdg.)